Pippa & Percival Pancake & Poppy

Four Peppy Puppies

By Deborah Diesen and Illustrated by Grace Zong

A puppy named Poppy
Went out for a run,
Tumbling, rumbling,
Looking for fun.

She came to a fence.
She heard a big sound.
She dug a hole under,
And that's when she found . . .

Another puppy!

Pancake and Poppy
Paraded along,
Gleeful and playful,
Their puppy legs strong.

They came to a stump.
They heard a big sound.
They clambered up over,
And that's when they found . . .

Another puppy!

Percival, Pancake,
And Poppy as one
Rollicked and frolicked
And raced in the sun.

They came to a heap.
They heard a big sound.
They pushed their way through,
And that's when they found . . .

Another puppy!

Pippa and Percival,
Pancake and Poppy,
Galloped and gamboled,
Their ears flippy-floppy.

They came to an alley.

They heard not a sound.

They squeezed their way in,

And that's when they found . . .

CLOSE
DANGE

A cat!!!!

Run, puppies, run!

Scoot and skedaddle!
Hotfoot and hurry!
Scramble and scuttle!
Scamper and scurry!

Four peppy puppies
Rushing away.
Done with adventure-
Enough for today!

They came to a sidewalk.
They sniffed all around.
They followed their noses,
And that's when they found . . .

Home!

PUPPY

For my friend Liza
–Debbie

For Agnes and Jessica
–Grace

Sleeping Bear Press™
2395 South Huron Parkway, Suite 200
Ann Arbor, MI 48104
www.sleepingbearpress.com

Printed and bound in the United States.

10 9 8 7 6 5 4 3 2 1

Library of Congress Cataloging-in-Publication Data

Names: Diesen, Deborah, author. | Zong, Grace, illustrator.
Title: Pippa and Percival, Pancake and Poppy: Four Peppy Puppies / written by Deborah Diesen; illustrated by Grace Zong.
Description: Ann Arbor, MI : Sleeping Bear Press, [2018] | Summary: Poppy the puppy meets three other pups while out for a run, but a surprise they find in a quiet alley sends them scrambling for home in this rhyming tale.
Identifiers: LCCN 2017029814 | ISBN 9781585363865
Subjects: | CYAC: Stories in rhyme. | Dogs—Fiction. | Animals—Infancy—Fiction.
Classification: LCC PZ8.3.D565 Fou 2018 | DDC [E]—dc23
LC record available at https://lccn.loc.gov/2017029814